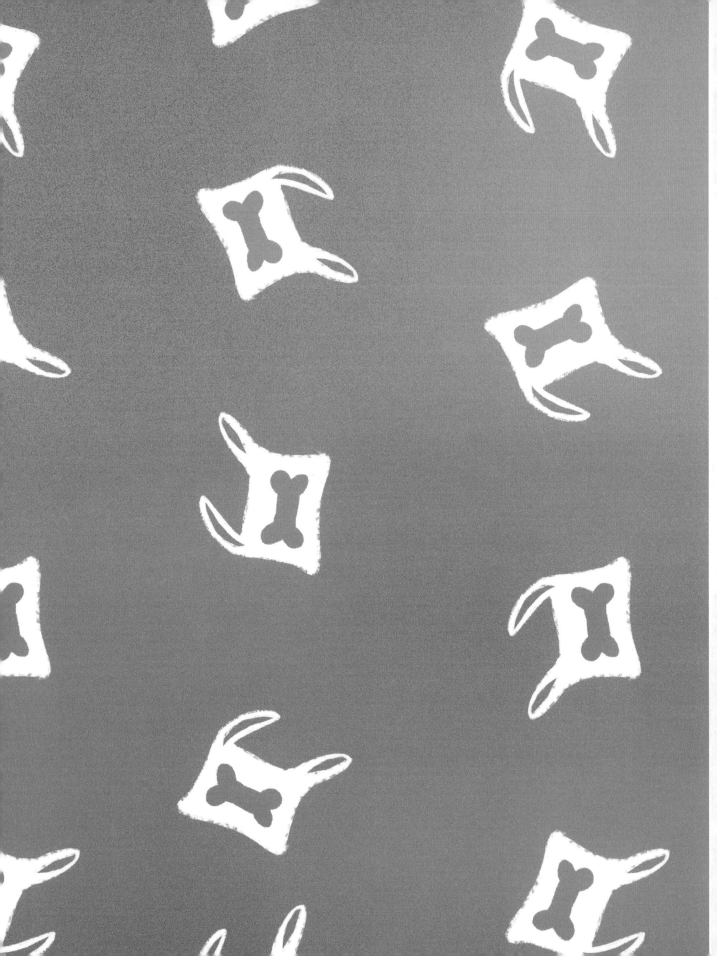

For my beautiful goddaughter
Isabella Rose, my angel on earth.

For Daddy, my angel above.
Your legacy lives on.

MASCOT
KIDS!

www.mascotbooks.com

BUSTER and THE BRAIN BULLY

For more information, please contact:
Mascot Books
620 Herndon Parkway, Suite 320
Herndon, VA 20170
info@mascotbooks.com

Library of Congress Control Number: 2020919357

CPSIA Code: PRT0521A
ISBN-13: 978-1-64543-828-1

Printed in the United States

BuSTeR
AND THE BRAIN BULLY

Christina Pellegrino

Illustrated by Teresa Alberini

My name is Buster, and I've got a bully in my bRaiN.
It's like mud in my mind, and it can be a real PaiN.

It makes me worry about
all kinds of STUFF;

it can make my day
pretty RUFF.

To you, it may seem super Silly,
but for me, I shake like I'm really Chilly.
I get scared of the thunder OutSide;
I pace around and try to hide.

The worry just won't go away;
I really wish I could just feel okay.
I try and I try, until suddenly one hour,
I think, HEY, I'll turn my fear into a SUPERPOWER!

I've heard about what therapy dogs do.
I think that's something I'd be good at, TOO!
I'll show my Brain Bully I am STRONG;
it isn't welcome here for long!

My Brain Bully shows up at the TEST.

First thunder, now this— WOOF! Bully, give it a REST!

But I focus hard, acing each and every **task**.
(And yes, I passed—I thought you might **ask!**)

I start visiting places—my job is so COOl!
One of my favorites is going to SChOOl.
I meet tons of kids—it's lots of FUN!
Though, I notice, not for EVERYONE.

I meet a friend who's really sad.
This makes me feel super bad.
She tells me, "Buster, I just don't get this book,"
and she has the most puzzled look.

Don't worry, I think, *I've got a Brain Bully,* TOO!
What does your Brain Bully do?
"It laughs at me when I try to READ;
I just can't keep up with the other kids' SPEED."

You can read to me at your own *PACE;*
don't worry, it's not a *RACE!*
I won't laugh, I can't *READ—*
a *SLOWER* speed might be just what we *NEED!*

So, the little girl sits next to ME, and opens her book so that I can SEE.

She starts to read and gets stuck on a WORD; I wait patiently as she figures it out . . .

"BUh—bRR—biRd!"

Believe
in
yourself

Another place my work takes ME
is to the hospital, where no kid wants to be.
I meet tons of kids, but they aren't having fun;
and, I notice, especially not this next one.

I meet a friend who's really sad.
This makes me feel super bad.
He tells me, "Buster, I am in in one foul mood,
and I can't stand the hospital food!"

Don't worry, I think, *I've got a Brain Bully*, TOO.
What does your Brain Bully do?
"I'm scared of the hospital, I want to go hOME,
but I've got this stupid broken bONE."

You can pet me for a whilE;
maybe that will make you SMile.
In time your bone will hEal,
then you can have a nice home-cooked MEal.

So, the teenage boy sits up in his bed,
and reaches over to pet my head.
He starts to smile and gives up the food fight;
I watch as he decides to take a small bite.

THUNDER, a TEST, a book, a broken bone . . .
Brain Bullies? Sorry, you've been OUTGROWN!
We all had courage and faced each of our FEARS,
look closely, now—we're ALL gathered right HERE:

A little girl reading a book on her OWN,
a teenage boy practicing on his crutches at home,
and a dog (that's me!) watching them with pure bliss.
It's a Magical moment you don't want to MISS!

My name is Buster and my superpower is to connect with love,
to help all kinds of kids see what they're really made of.
You have your own superpower, too,
so show your Brain Bully what you can do!

HERE'S WHAT THE KIDS I WORK WITH have TO SAY. HOW AMAZING ARE THEY?

"When I go read to Buster, I'm so excited. I feel good when I read to him. I do good when I read with him. I look forward to every Tuesday when I go to meet Buster."

BRIANNA

"Reading to Buster is amazing! My mom won't let me get a dog, so Buster is that substitute for me. I look forward every week to seeing him and spending time with him. And I love reading picture books to him as I hope he can understand and enjoy the pictures. Thank you so much for the weeks and months of happiness!"

CHARLOTTE

"Reading to Buster is so much fun! I love reading Buster stories I have written in class. Buster is always a good listener."
Leighton

"I like reading to Buster because he listens to me. Buster is the kindest dog."
Silvia

"I enjoyed reading to Buster and it always made me happy. I had fun reading the dog books with Buster."
Andrew

"It is fun to read to Buster. I like to pet him while I read. I like to read dog books to Buster."
Adriana

"Reading to Buster is fun! I always like seeing Buster."
William

About the Author

Buster is a ten-year-old golden retriever and one half of a therapy-dog team with his owner, Christina. This book was inspired by their work in the hospital, school, and library settings. Buster and Christina are passionate about making a difference in the world of mental health, and they are strong believers in the power of the human-animal connection. The duo works with Bright and Beautiful Therapy Dogs, as well as Reading Education Assistance Dogs® (R.E.A.D.®).

@Busters.borough
therapyanimals.org/R.E.A.D.html

BUSTER'S BRAIN BREAK

I'd like to take a paws to appreciate a friend or two.
They work behind the scenes; here's what these incredible people do:

COMPASSIONATE CLAIRE:

Our production editor who has been there every step of the way.
She just gets it—what more can I say?

TALENTED TERESA:

Our illustrator who captured my look with such ease.
All the way from Italy, she is sure to please!

Thank you for believing in our dream.
We couldn't have asked for a better team!

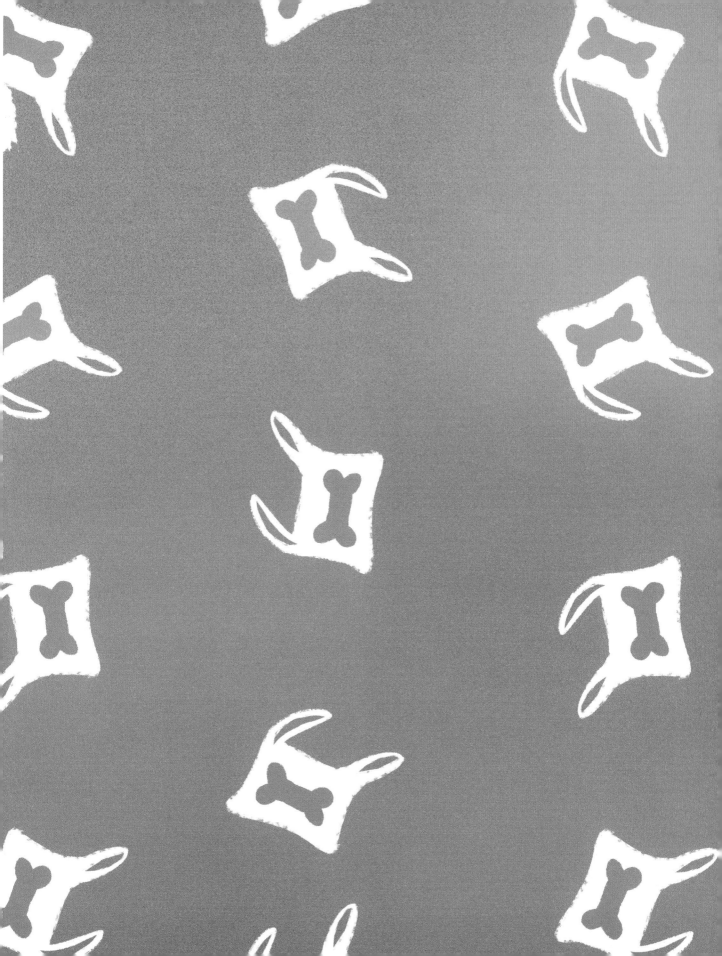